Dear Parent:
Your child's love of reading starts here!

Every child learns to read in a different way and at his or her own speed. Some go back and forth between reading levels and read favorite books again and again. Others read through each level in order. You can help your young reader improve and become more confident by encouraging his or her own interests and abilities. From books your child reads with you to the first books he or she reads alone, there are I Can Read Books for every stage of reading:

SHARED READING
Basic language, word repetition, and whimsical illustrations, ideal for sharing with your emergent reader

BEGINNING READING
Short sentences, familiar words, and simple concepts for children eager to read on their own

READING WITH HELP
Engaging stories, longer sentences, and language play for developing readers

READING ALONE
Complex plots, challenging vocabulary, and high-interest topics for the independent reader

ADVANCED READING
Short paragraphs, chapters, and exciting themes for the perfect bridge to chapter books

I Can Read Books have introduced children to the joy of reading since 1957. Featuring award-winning authors and illustrators and a fabulous cast of beloved characters, I Can Read Books set the standard for beginning readers.

A lifetime of discovery begins with the magical words **"I Can Read!"**

Visit www.icanread.com for information
on enriching your child's reading experience.

This one's for Mandy, too.

Balzer + Bray is an imprint of HarperCollins Publishers.
I Can Read Book® is a trademark of HarperCollins Publishers.

Fox the Tiger
Copyright © 2018 by Corey R. Tabor
All rights reserved. Manufactured in the U.S.A.
No part of this book may be used or reproduced in any manner whatsoever without written permission except
in the case of brief quotations embodied in critical articles and reviews. For information address HarperCollins
Children's Books, a division of HarperCollins Publishers, 195 Broadway, New York, NY 10007.
www.icanread.com

Library of Congress Control Number: 2017902783
ISBN 978-0-06-239869-7 (trade bdg.) — ISBN 978-0-06-239867-3 (pbk.)

The artist used pencil, watercolor, and crayon, assembled digitally, to create the illustrations for this book.
Typography by Dana Fritts
Title hand lettering by Alexandra Snowdon
20 21 22 CWM 15 14 13
❖
First Edition

I Can Read! — SHARED My First READING

FOX
the
TIGER

By Corey R. Tabor

BALZER + BRAY

An Imprint of HarperCollins Publishers

"I wish I were a tiger,"

says Fox.

"Tigers are big.

Tigers are fast.

Tigers are sneaky.

Tigers are the best."

Fox has an idea.

"There. Now I am a tiger,"
says Tiger.

Tiger goes for a prowl.

"Hello, Fox," says Turtle.

"I am not Fox.

I am Tiger," says Tiger.

"I prowl and growl."

Now Turtle has an idea.

"Wait here," says Turtle.

14

Tiger waits.

"Hi, Turtle," says Tiger.

"Hi, Turtle," says Rabbit.

"I am not Turtle.

I am Race Car," says Race Car.

"I zip and zoom."

Now Rabbit has an idea.

"Wait here," says Rabbit.

Tiger waits.

Race Car waits, too.

"Hi, Rabbit," says Tiger.

"Hi, Rabbit," says Race Car.

"I am not Rabbit.

I am Robot," says Robot.

"I *beep bop boop.*"

Tiger prowls and growls!

Race Car zips and zooms!

Robot *beep bop boops!*

Drip, drop, drip, drop.

It starts to rain.

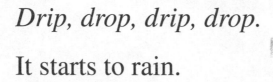

Soon Turtle is Turtle,

Rabbit is Rabbit,

and Fox is Fox.

"Oh well," says Turtle.

"Oh well," says Rabbit.

They go in from the rain.

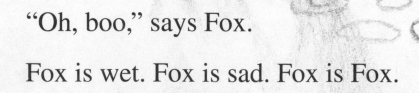

"Oh, boo," says Fox.

Fox is wet. Fox is sad. Fox is Fox.

"Wow! A fox!" says Squirrel.

"Foxes are big!

Foxes are fast!

Foxes are sneaky!

Foxes are the best!"

"Yes," says Turtle.

"Foxes are the best!"

Fox smiles. Fox is glad

to be a fox.